An I Can Read Book®

# The Josefina Story Quilt

## By Eleanor Coerr

## Pictures by Bruce Degen

HarperCollins Publishers

HarperCollins®, ☕®, and I Can Read Book® are
trademarks of HarperCollins Publishers Inc.

The Josefina Story Quilt
Text copyright © 1986 by Eleanor Coerr
Illustrations copyright © 1986 by Bruce Degen
Printed in the U.S.A. All rights reserved.
www.harperchildrens.com

Library of Congress Cataloging-in-Publication Data
Coerr, Eleanor.
The Josefina story quilt.
    p.    cm. — (An I can read book)
    Summary: While traveling west with her family in
1850, a young girl makes a patchwork quilt chronicling
the experiences of the journey and reserves two special
patches for her pet hen Josefina.
    ISBN 0-06-021348-5 — ISBN 0-06-021349-3 (lib. bdg.)
    ISBN 0-06-444129-6 (pbk.)
    [1. Quilting—Fiction.    2. Chickens—Fiction.
3. Overland journeys to the Pacific—Fiction.]    I. Degen,
Bruce, ill.    II. Title.    III. Series.
PZ7.C6567Jo    1986                        85-45260
[E]

# Contents

# Josefina

It was May 1850.

Faith was excited.

They were going to California

in a covered wagon.

"Please," Faith asked Ma,

"can I take Josefina?"

Josefina was her pet hen

and Faith loved her.

She liked the way Josefina

snuggled in her arms.

She liked the way Josefina

followed her around.

Ma was baking bread

for the long journey.

"Ask your Pa," she said.

Pa and Faith's brother, Adam,
were loading the wagon.

"Please, Pa," Faith said,
"please can I take Josefina?"

"There is no room in the wagon
for pets," Pa said.

"That isn't fair," said Faith.

8

"Adam can bring his colt."

"A colt is not a pet," said Pa.

"A colt can carry a load of corn."

"What can Josefina do?"

teased Adam.

"She is too old to lay eggs

and too tough to eat."

Faith's eyes filled with tears.

She ran back to the house.

Ma sat down in the rocker

and held Faith on her lap.

"We all must leave things behind,"

she said gently.

"I love this rocker,

but there is no room for it

in the wagon."

Faith gulped down her sobs.

"I have looked after Josefina

since she was a little chick,"

she said.

"What will happen to her?"

"Perhaps a neighbor
will take her," said Ma.
But nobody wanted a hen
that was too old to lay eggs
and too tough to eat.

# California, Ho!

Early in the morning

the wagon was ready.

It had blue trim

and a white cloth roof.

Ma stood back to admire it.

"A big flowerpot on wheels!"

she said.

"Isn't it beautiful?"

Faith did not answer.

She was worried about Josefina.

"Did you pack the food?"

Ma asked Pa.

"And my kitchen things?"

Pa nodded.

"Then that is everything

except the bedding," said Ma.

Faith thought sadly,

"And Josefina."

Pa threw mattresses

into the wagon.

Ma carefully spread

their patchwork quilts over them.

17

"We can't leave these behind,"
she said.

"All our joys and sorrows
are sewn up into the patches."

Faith picked up Josefina

and held her close.

"We can't leave my hen, either,"

she said.

"Josefina MUST stay!" Pa said.

"So put her down."

Faith just stood there.

She stroked Josefina's feathers

and tried hard not to cry.

Ma gave Pa a special look.

Pa sighed.

"All right, Faith," he said.

"But if she makes any trouble,

OUT SHE GOES!"

"Thank you, Pa!" cried Faith.

"She will be good, I promise."

Faith put Josefina in her cage.

Pa hung it high up

at the back of the wagon.

Then he lifted Faith

up next to it.

Ma handed her the ragbag.

"Work on a patch

whenever you can," she said.

Faith knew how important

quilts were for remembering.

"California, ho!" shouted Pa.

He snapped his long whip.

C R A A A A C K!

The oxen began to move.

Their bells tinkled.

The heavy wagon chains clanked.

And the wheels began

their creaky song.

25

Faith smiled happily at Josefina.

This would be their home

on the long trail West.

Faith took some calico

from the ragbag.

"I will make my first

wagon train patch," she said.

Faith began to sew a wagon wheel

with careful, tiny stitches.

# Trouble

At night

the wagons made a circle

around the animals.

Women cooked the meals

over a campfire.

Afterward,

there was singing and banjo music.

Faith put down

the wagon wheel patch

and let Josefina out for a stretch.

Suddenly,

"W O O O O F!"

A dog ran up to Josefina

and barked fiercely at her.

Josefina squawked and ran.

"Come back!" yelled Faith.

But it was too late.

Josefina was in the middle

of the animals.

Horses snorted and reared.

Cows kicked and mooed.

Oxen bellowed.

"That pesky hen!" Pa shouted,

and ran after her.

"She almost started a stampede,"

Pa said angrily.

"OUT SHE GOES!"

"Please, Pa," begged Faith,

"give her one more chance.

It was the dog's fault."

"Faith is right," said Ma.

"I saw the whole thing."

Pa put Josefina back in her cage.

"Just one more chance," he said.

That night, Faith whispered,

"Josefina, please try to be good."

"Cluck!…Cluck!…Cluck!"

said the hen.

They understood one another

as true friends do.

# The Rescue

For a long time

Josefina was good.

She quietly watched Faith

sew patches for the quilt.

She didn't make a sound

when hail beat down on the roof,

or when spring rains blew in

and soaked her feathers.

She made just a little cluck

when coyotes howled at night.

But how Josefina fussed

when they crossed rivers!

One day they came

to a wide, muddy river.

Josefina made so much noise

that Faith had to take her

out of the cage.

She held her close.

"It's all right," Faith crooned.

Pa was driving the oxen into the river,
when S Q U O O O O S H!

A back wheel sank into a hole.

Faith let go of Josefina.

Josefina fell into the river.

The current carried her away.

"Help!" cried Faith.

"Save Josefina!"

Adam jumped into the river,

but the current was too strong.

It took three men

to get them out.

"That does it!" Pa shouted.

"She is too old to lay eggs,

too tough to eat,

and she falls into rivers.

OUT SHE GOES!"

Just then

Josefina ruffled her feathers,

let out a proud

"Caaaa—CACKLE—ackle!"

and laid a beautiful big white egg.

"By thunder!" Pa said.

"She has begun to lay eggs again."

"Wonderful!" said Ma.

"Now we will have fresh eggs."

So Josefina stayed.

Faith found a white scrap

for the egg patch.

# Robbers!

Spring turned into summer.

The desert was hot and dry.

Faith counted her patches.

Now she had fifteen.

It was time to sew one

about the desert.

But one bad thing

came after another.

Wagon wheels kept falling off.

There was not enough food

for the animals.

Then three oxen died.

Pa had to throw out his heavy tools

and Ma's black iron stove.

Two old people died.

They were buried

beside the trail.

Nobody laughed or sang

or smiled anymore.

Faith was always hungry,

but she walked on and on.

She looked for grain or seeds

for Josefina.

It was worse in the hills.

The trail was rocky and steep.

One morning Indians came to trade

buffalo meat and water.

They wanted Ma's quilts.

"Never!" said Ma.

"I would rather starve."

They wanted Josefina.

"Never!" cried Faith.

"I would rather die."

So Pa traded extra clothes

for food and water.

Everyone felt better

after a good meal.

Soon the food was gone.

"If those Indians come back,"

Pa told Faith,

"we must trade Josefina for water."

Faith prayed hard

that they would never return.

The night was bitter cold.

Men slept under the wagons.

Ma gave the quilts

to Pa and Adam.

She and Faith

bundled in old blankets.

About midnight

two robbers crept into camp.

They sneaked up to the wagon.

When they reached for the quilts,

Josefina heard them.

"CACKLE! CACKLE! CACKLE!"

she squawked.

Everyone woke up

and the robbers ran away.

Pa laughed for the first time

in days.

"Josefina may be old," he said,

"but she is a humdinger

of a watchdog."

# Good-bye, Josefina

Pa reached for the cage

to thank Josefina,

but the poor old hen

was lying on the cage floor.

Faith hid her face against Ma.

"You must be brave,"

Ma said softly.

"Josefina lived a good long life."

"You can be proud of her,"

Pa added.

"She died helping us," said Adam.

Faith did not feel better.

She cried and cried.

Ma hugged her

for a long time.

The next morning

they had a funeral for Josefina.

Faith wrapped her

in the prettiest scrap of cloth.

Adam buried her

under a tall pine tree.

"I miss her so!"

Faith said between sobs.

At last Faith dried her eyes

and reached for the ragbag.

"I will sew a pine tree patch

for Josefina," she said.

Soon the wagon train

found food and water.

When they reached California,

Faith finished the patches.

Pa built a quilting frame
in their new cabin.

The family helped Faith
stitch the patches together
into a quilt.

The quilt covered Faith's bed.

Every day the patches
helped them remember
the good times
and the bad times
on the wagon train.

And every night

Faith felt warm and happy

under the Josefina story quilt.

# Author's Note

In the mid 1800s, thousands of pioneers traveled to the West in covered wagons to find a better life. They usually began their journeys in the spring, from frontier towns in Missouri. Families joined together to form wagon trains so that they could protect and help each other. The trip to California took about six months.

Each wagon was loaded down with food, cooking pots, tools, clothes, and furniture. It took five or six pairs of strong oxen to pull one. The families traveled twelve to fifteen miles each day across dangerous rivers, hot deserts, and steep, rocky trails.

There was no school, but children had chores to do. Women and girls knitted, mended clothes, or sewed quilts.

Patchwork quilts were given as gifts for babies, birthdays, and weddings. The most beautiful quilts won prizes at county fairs and were precious to their owners.

In those days, a quilt was often the family's diary. Many patterns that are still used today, such as the wagon wheel, star over Texas, log cabin, and cactus flower, originated from wagon train living.

Some of our museums show patchwork quilts as old as the Josefina story quilt.